ADELINA'S WHALES

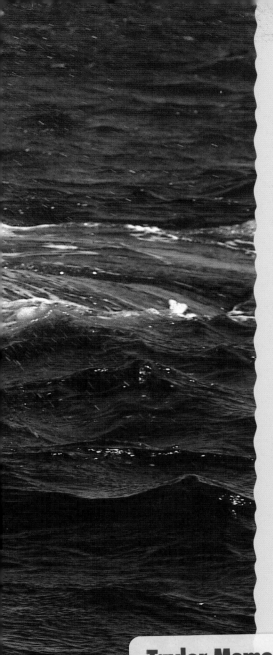

ADELINA'S WHALES

text and photographs by RICHARD SOBOL

DUTTON CHILDREN'S BOOKS   New York

Taylor Memorial Public Library
Cuyahoga Falls, Ohio

Text and photographs copyright © 2003 by Richard Sobol
All rights reserved.

CIP Data is available.

Published in the United States
by Dutton Children's Books,
a division of Penguin Putnam Books for Young Readers
345 Hudson Street, New York, New York 10014
www.penguinputnam.com

Designed by Irene Vandervoort

Manufactured in China
First Edition
10 9 8 7 6 5 4 3 2 1

ISBN 0-525-47110-3

FOREWORD

When I first visited Laguna San Ignacio, this gray whale nursery was in trouble. I had traveled to this remote corner of Mexico in the spring of 1997 with the film artists Glenn Close and Pierce Brosnan and with environmental leaders in order to protest the plan of a powerful multi-national corporation to build the world's largest salt-producing factory there. The corporation intended to flood an area twice the size of Washington, D.C., and produce millions of gallons of wastewater. Mexican groups had asked my organization—the National Resources Defense Council (NRDC)—to help them block this project.

Many of us brought our children on that first trip to see the whales. I arrived with my eight-year-old daughter, Kick, and was instantly enthralled with the stark beauty of the Baja desert. The whales seemed especially taken by Kick, her best friend, Annie, and their young pal Sean. When Kick, Annie, and Sean dunked their heads over the gunnel of our small panga (fishing boat), the giant mammals were apparently drawn by the sounds of their laughter. They schooled around our boats, turning their heads to gaze at us with their smart, soft eyes, and opened their giant mouths for us to stroke their baleen and tongues, which they particularly enjoyed. The ancestors of human beings evolved side by side with the ancestors of whales until the whales returned to the water millions of years ago. During these intimate contacts in Laguna San Ignacio, both of us—whales and humans—seemed to recall our distant brotherhood at the dawn of creation. Like Adelina, Kick and I and all our friends experienced a kind of primal bliss from these encounters.

One day, I drove to the nearby village of La Laguna to dive for hatchet clams with fishermen like Adelina's father, Runolfo, and her grandfather Pachico. Fraying ropes held the noisy antique gasoline-powered air pump to the center thwart of our panga. Donning heavy boots and weight belts, we hiked the bottom of the lagoon, using long air hoses to breathe, harpooning the giant clams. As we sat shucking our catch in the tiny boat, the fishermen told me they did not want to see the clean waters of the lagoon turned into an industrial dumping ground. After hearing their concerns, I was determined to help the people of Baja to protect Laguna San Ignacio. These fishermen knew the lesson that Adelina and my daughter Kick understood instinctively—humans don't have the right to destroy what we cannot create.

In March 2000, after nearly a million people had written letters of protest, the Mexican government and the corporation announced that the saltworks was permanently canceled. Richard Sobol's photographs convey the importance of this victory. They were an integral part of the efforts to save Laguna San Ignacio.

The struggle to protect the planet's last remaining wilderness areas continues through NRDC's BioGems program. Through the BioGems Web site (www.savebiogems.org), students and teachers can learn more about these special gems—places that are home to rare and endangered wildlife, like Adelina's whales—and what they can do to help protect them.

ROBERT F. KENNEDY, JR.

La Laguna is the name of a quiet, dusty fishing village on the sandy shore of Laguna San Ignacio, in Baja California, Mexico. A few dozen homesites are scattered along the water's edge. These little houses are simple one- or two-room boxes patched together with plywood and sheet metal. Drinking water is stored outside in fifty-gallon plastic barrels, and electricity is turned on for only a few hours each day.

Adelina Mayoral has lived her whole life in La Laguna. She is a bright ten-year-old girl. She loves the ocean and the feeling of the ever-present wind that blows her long, dark hair into wild tangles. She knows what time of day it is by looking at the way the light reflects off the water. Adelina can tell what month it is by watching the kind of birds that nest in the mangroves behind her home. She can even recognize when it is low tide. Simply by taking a deep breath through her nose, she can smell the clams and seaweed that bake in the hot sun on the shoreline as the water level goes down.

In late January, every afternoon after school, Adelina walks to the beach to see if her friends—the gray whales—have returned. At this same time every year the whales come, traveling from as far away as Alaska and Russia. They slowly and steadily swim south, covering more than five thousand miles along the Pacific Coast during November, December, and January.

One night Adelina is awakened by a loud, low, rumbling noise. It is the sound of a forty-ton gray whale exhaling a room-size blast of hot wet air. As she has always known they would, the gray whales have come again to visit. Adelina smiles and returns to her sleep, comforted by the sounds of whales breathing and snoring outside her window. At daybreak she runs to the lagoon and sees two clouds of mist out over the water, the milky trails of breath left by a mother gray whale and her newborn calf.

The waters of the protected lagoon are warm and shallow. The scientists who have come to visit and study the whales have explained that Laguna San Ignacio is the perfect place for the mother whales to have their babies and then teach them how to swim. But Adelina knows why they really come — to visit her!

Adelina's family lives far away from big cities with highways and shopping malls. Her little village does not have any movie theaters or traffic lights, but she knows that her hometown is a special place. This is the only place on earth where these giant gray whales—totally wild animals—choose to seek out the touch of a human hand. Only here in Laguna San Ignacio do whales ever stop swimming and say hello to their human neighbors. Raising their massive heads up out of the water, they come face-to-face with people. Some mother whales even lift their newborns up on their backs to help them get a better view of those who have come to see them. Or maybe they are just showing off, sharing their new baby the way any proud parent would.

The whales have been coming to this lagoon for hundreds of years, and Adelina is proud that her grandfather, Pachico, was the first person to tell of a "friendly" visit with one. She loves to hear him tell the story of that whale and that day. She listens closely as he talks about being frightened, since he didn't know then that the whale was only being friendly. He thought he was in big trouble.

Adelina looks first at the tight, leathery skin of her grandfather, browned from his many years of fishing in the bright tropical sun. From his face she glances down to the small plastic model of a gray whale that he keeps close by. As he begins to tell the story of his first friendly whale encounter, there is a twinkle in his eye and a large smile on his face. Adelina and her father, Runolfo, smile too, listening again to the story that they have heard so many times before.

In a whisper, her grandfather begins to draw them in. Adelina closes her eyes to imagine the calm and quiet on that first afternoon when his small boat was gently nudged by a huge gray whale. As the boat rocked, her grandfather and his fishing partner's hearts pounded. They held tight and waited, preparing themselves to be thrown into the water by the giant animal. The whale dove below them and surfaced again on the opposite side of their boat, scraping her head along the smooth sides. Instead of being tossed from the boat, they were surprised to find themselves still upright and floating. For the next hour the whale glided alongside them, bumping and bobbing gently—as gently as possible for an animal that is as long as a school bus and as wide as a soccer goal. As the sun started to set behind them, the whale gave out a great blast of wet, snotty saltwater that soaked their clothes and stuck to their skin. The whale then rose up inches away from their boat and dove into the sea. Her first visit was over.

As her grandfather finishes the story, he looks to Adelina, who joins him in speaking the last line of the story:

"Well, my friend, no fish today!" they say before breaking into laughter.

After this first friendly visit with the whales, word quickly spread of the unique encounter between a wild fifty-foot whale and a tiny fishing boat. Scientists and whale watchers started to come to Laguna San Ignacio to see the whales themselves. Perhaps word spread among the whales, too, because now dozens of whales began to approach the small boats. With brains as large as a car's engine, gray whales might even have their own language. They "talk" in low rumbles and loud clicks, making noises that sound like the tappings of a steel drum or the ticking that a playing card makes as it slaps against the spokes of a turning bicycle wheel. Maybe they told each other that it was safe to visit here.

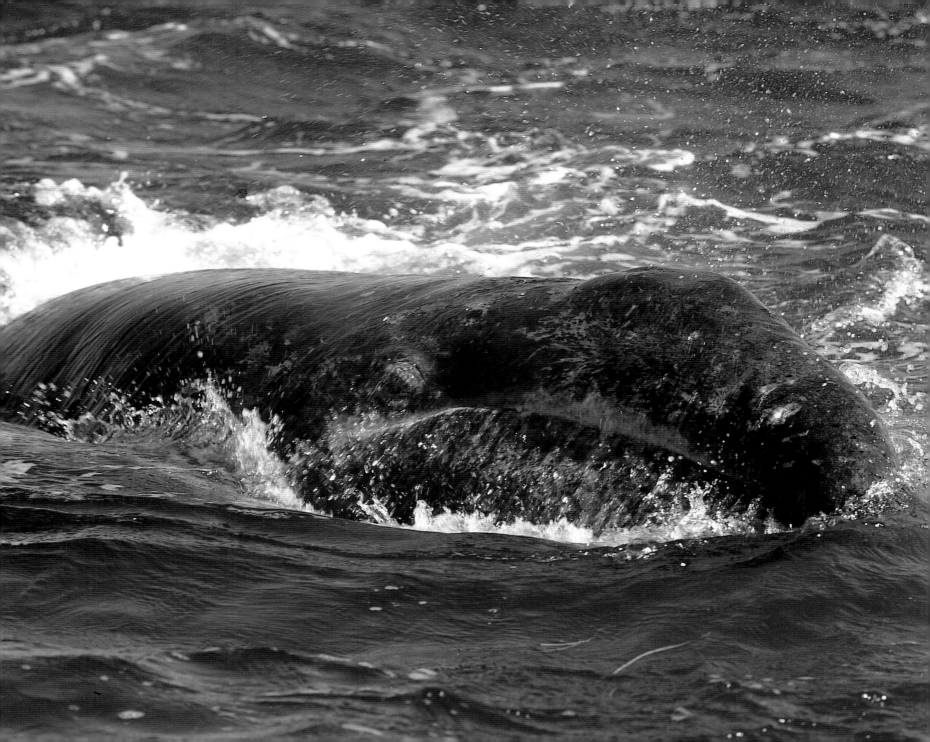

Adelina's favorite time of the day is the late afternoon, when her father and grand-father return from their trips on the water, guiding visitors to see the whales. They sit together as the sun goes down behind them, and she listens to stories of the whales. She asks them lots and lots of questions.

Adelina has learned a lot about the gray whales. She knows that when a whale leaps out of the water and makes a giant splash falling back in, it's called breaching. When a whale pops its head straight up out of the water, as if it is looking around to see what is going on, it is called spyhopping. Adelina also learned how the whale's wide, flat tail is called a fluke, and when it raises its tail up in the air as it goes into a deep dive, that is called fluking.

Although her home is a simple shack on a sandy bluff hugging the edge of the Pacific Ocean, Adelina has many new friends who come to share her world. She has met people who come from beyond the end of the winding, bumpy road that rings the lagoon. Some are famous actors. Some are politicians. Some speak Spanish. Some speak English. Those that weigh forty tons speak to her in their own magical style. The whales have taught her that the world is a big place.

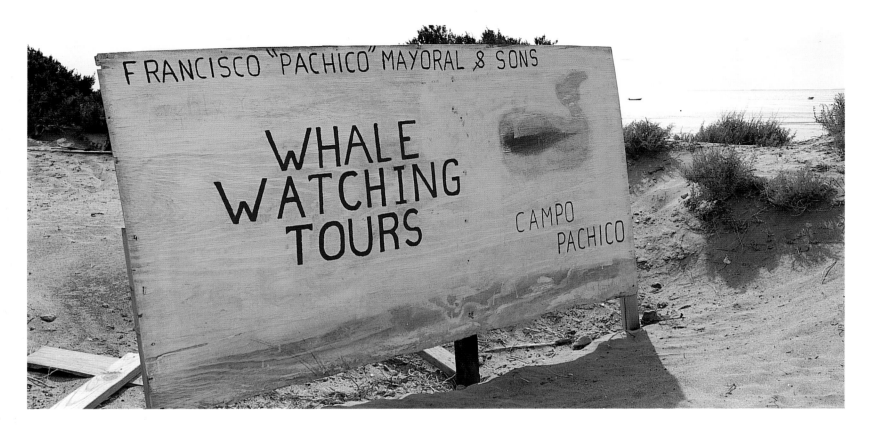

Adelina knows that she has many choices in her future. Sometimes she giggles with delight at the idea of being the first girl to captain a panga (a small open fishing boat) and teach people about the whales in the lagoon. Or sometimes she thinks she may become a biologist who studies the ocean and can one day help to unlock some of the mysteries of the whales in her own backyard. Or maybe she will take pictures like the photographer whom she watches juggling his three cameras as he stumbles aboard the whale-watching boat. But no matter what she chooses, the whales will always be a part of her life.

For these three months Adelina knows how lucky she is to live in Laguna San Ignacio, the little corner of Mexico that the gray whales choose for their winter home. This is the place where two worlds join together. She wouldn't trade it for anything.

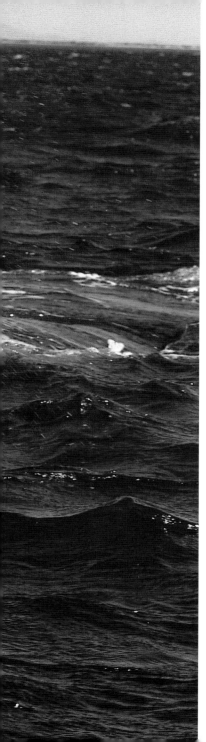

In the early spring the lagoon grows quiet. One by one the whales swim off, heading north for a summer of feeding. On their heads and backs they carry the fingerprints of those they met, the memories of their encounters in Mexico. Maybe, as the whales sleep, they dream of the colorful sunsets of Laguna San Ignacio.

Every afternoon Adelina continues to gaze across the water. Sometimes now, when she closes her eyes, she can still see the whales swimming by. And if she listens *really* closely, she can even hear their breathing.

ABOUT THE GRAY WHALES

SCIENTIFIC NAME: *Eschrichtius robustus*

SIZE: Gray whales grow to be thirty-five to fifty feet long and weigh between twenty and forty tons. Newborn calves have an average length of fifteen feet and weigh 1,500 pounds. Newborns will nurse on fifty gallons of mother's milk each day for six or seven months as they grow quickly and double in weight.

LIFE SPAN: Average life is thirty to forty years, but it can be as long as sixty years.

FEEDING: Gray whales are toothless. This type of whale is called a baleen whale. Baleen is the name for the flexible hornlike substance that forms the fringed plates that hang like curtains from the whale's upper jaw. This stringy material is made from keratin, the same material that makes up fingernails on humans. Gray whales feed from the ocean bottom, sucking in huge amounts of seawater. As they force the water back out from their mouths, the baleen acts like a filter, allowing the water to pass through but trapping all the small animals and shrimp. Each gulp gives the whale many pounds of vitamin-rich food.

POPULATION: There are now more than twenty thousand gray whales in the Pacific Ocean. They were hunted until 1946 and were then thought to number less than two thousand. They have made one of the most dramatic recoveries of any threatened species.

PREDATORS: They are hunted by orcas (killer whales) and large sharks.

HABITAT: Gray whales spend the warm summer months in the northernmost range of the Pacific Ocean in both Alaska and Russia. As the days grow short in October, they head south on an almost six-thousand-mile migration. Traveling in small groups of up to twelve animals, they reach the warm waters of Baja California, Mexico, in January. They remain in Mexico for three months before heading north again.